This book belongs to:

. . . .

. . . .

For Sally and Wembury Beach,
and to Peter and Margaret Bryan,
Karen, Jacqui and Alison,
with love

To find out more about
Simon James and his books visit
www.simonjamesbooks.com

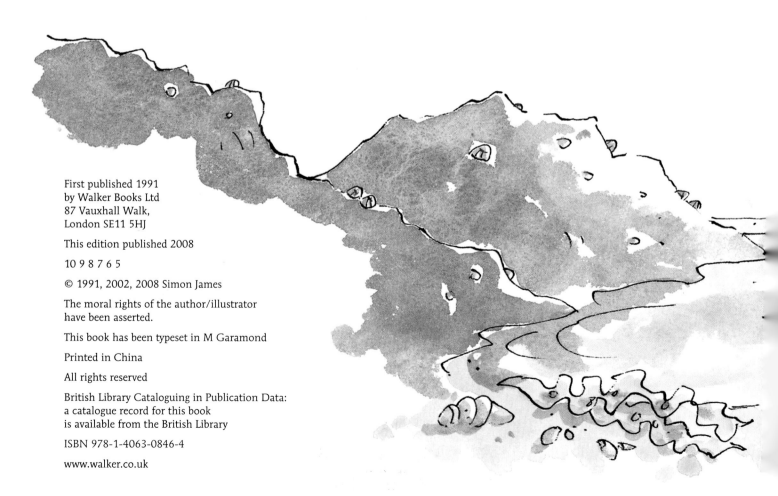

First published 1991
by Walker Books Ltd
87 Vauxhall Walk,
London SE11 5HJ

This edition published 2008

10 9 8 7 6 5

© 1991, 2002, 2008 Simon James

The moral rights of the author/illustrator
have been asserted.

This book has been typeset in M Garamond

Printed in China

British Library Cataloguing in Publication Data:
a catalogue record for this book
is available from the British Library

ISBN 978-1-4063-0846-4

www.walker.co.uk

SIMON JAMES

Sally
and the
Limpet

WALKER BOOKS
AND SUBSIDIARIES
LONDON · BOSTON · SYDNEY · AUCKLAND

Not long ago, on a Sunday, Sally was down on the beach exploring, when she found a

brightly coloured, bigger-than-usual limpet shell.
She wanted to take it home but, as she pulled,

the limpet made a little squelching noise
and held on to the rock.

The harder Sally tugged, the more tightly
the limpet held on,

until, suddenly, Sally slipped and
fell – with the limpet now stuck to her finger.

Though she pulled with all her might, it just wouldn't come off. So she ran over to her dad.

He heaved and groaned, but the limpet made a little squelching noise and held on even tighter.

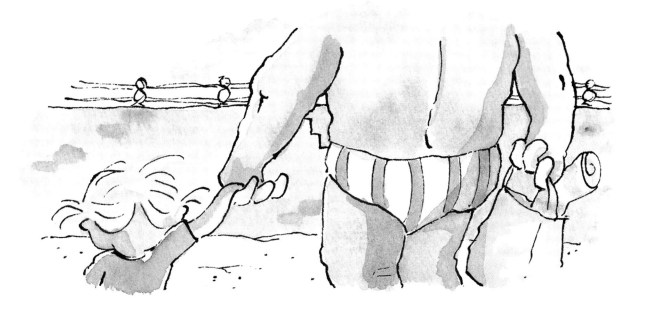

So, that afternoon, Sally went home in the
car with a limpet stuck to her finger.

When they got home, her dad tried using his tools.
Her brother tried offering it lettuce and cucumber.

But, that night, Sally went to bed with a
limpet stuck to her finger.

Next day it was school.

All her friends tried to pull the limpet off Sally's finger.
Mr Blueberry, the nature teacher,
said that limpets
live for twenty years,
and stay all their whole
lives on the
same rock.

In the afternoon, Sally's mother took her
to the hospital, to see the doctor.

He tried chemicals, injections, potions and pinchers.
Sally was beginning to feel upset.

Everyone was making
too much fuss all
around her.

She kicked over the doctor's chair and ran.

She ran through the endless corridors.
She just wanted to be on her own.

She ran out of the hospital and through the town.

She didn't stop when she got to the beach.

She ran through people's sandcastles.
She even ran over a big man.

When she reached the water, she jumped in
with all her clothes on.

Sally landed with a big splash

and then just sat quietly in the water.
The limpet, feeling at home once more,

made a little squelching noise and
wiggled off her finger.

But Sally didn't forget what Mr Blueberry,
the nature teacher, had said.

Very carefully, she lifted the limpet
by the top of its shell.
She carried it back across
the beach, past the
man she had
walked over,

and gently, so gently, she put the limpet back
on the very same rock where she had found it
the day before. Then, humming to herself,

she took the long way home across the beach.

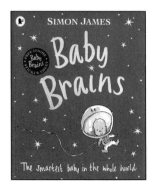
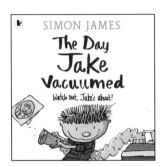
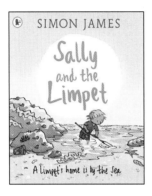
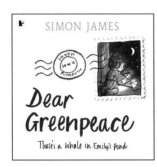

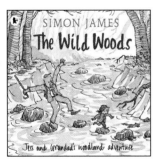